THE MARGARET ST. CLAIR
SCIENCE FICTION MEGAPACK®

THE MARGARET ST. CLAIR SCIENCE FICTION MEGAPACK®

MARGARET ST. CLAIR

WILDSIDE PRESS

CONTENTS

INTRODUCTION

Margaret St. Clair (1911–1995) was an American fantasy and science fiction writer, who also wrote under the pseudonyms Idris Seabright and Wilton Hazzard.

She was born as Eva Margaret Neeley in Hutchinson, Kansas. Her father, US Representative George A. Neeley, died when Margaret was seven, but left her mother well provided for. With no siblings, Margaret recalled her childhood as "rather a lonely and bookish one." When she was seventeen, she and her mother moved to California. In 1932, after graduating from the University of California, Berkeley, she married writer Eric St. Clair. In 1934 she earned a Master of Arts in Greek Classics. The St. Clairs lived in a hilltop house with a panoramic view in what is now El Sobrante, California, where Margaret gardened. She also bred and sold dachshund puppies.

In her rare autobiographical writings, Margaret St. Clair revealed few details of her personal life, but interviews with some who knew her indicate that she and her husband were well-traveled (including some visits to nudist colonies), were childless by choice, and in 1966 were initiated into Wicca by Raymond Buckland, taking the Craft names Froniga and Weyland. Eric St. Clair worked variously as a statistician, social worker, horticulturist, shopfitter, and a laboratory assistant in the University of California at Berkeley Physics Department. He also published numerous short stories and magazine articles and was "perhaps the leading American writer of children's stories about bears, having sold close to 100 of them," according to the introduction to his story "Olsen and the Sea Gul," which appeared in *The Magazine of Fantasy & Science Fiction*, (September 1964).

The St. Clairs eventually moved from El Sobrante to a house on the coast near Point Arena, "where every window had an ocean view." Margaret survived her husband by several years. A lifelong supporter of the American Friends Service Committee, she spent her final years at Friends House in Santa Rosa, California.

—John Betancourt
Cabin John, Maryland

FLOWERING EVIL

Originally published in *Planet Stories*, Summer 1950.

Captain Bjornson shook a grizzled head. "I never saw a plant I liked the looks of less," he said. "I don't know how he got it through the planetary plant quarantine. You take my advice, Amy, and watch out for it." He took another of the little geela nut cookies from the quaint old lucite platter, and bit into it appreciatively.

Mrs. Dinsmore sniffed, "I don't know what you're driving at," she said coldly, "or why you're so prejudiced against my poor little Rambler. You know perfectly well that Robert would never send me anything the least bit dangerous."

Captain Bjornson paused with another cookie half-way to his lips and looked at her. "Wouldn't send you anything dangerous!" he exclaimed. "Why, Amy, have you forgotten how your face was swelled up for two weeks from that tree cutting he sent you? The doctor said it was a contact poison worse than sumach, and he tried to get you to go to the hospital. What about the time that cactus from the Blue Desert went to seed, and I spent thirty-six hours picking spines out of you? What about—" Mrs. Dinsmore gave a warning sniff.

"Well, all right," Bjornson said. "I know how fond you are of Bob, and I know you don't like me to mention his mistakes. I'll grant you he means well. So what? He's flighty, scatter-brained, and brash. To use an expression that was current when I was a boy, Bob is a twerp."

Mrs. Dinsmore pulled the lucite platter so far over to her own side of the table that Bjornson couldn't get another cookie from it without getting up and stretching out along the table cloth. "I don't agree with you," she said distantly. "Robert is a splendid fellow, so thoughtful and considerate. He takes a real interest in my soap carvings, and how many young men with an important position like his, third mate on a space freighter with a regularly scheduled run, would remember to send back plants from every port of call to an aunt on earth? I shouldn't be surprised if I won a blue ribbon at the flower show again this year; my Golden Rain plant is about to bloom. Robert tells me it's a lovely thing."

The captain cast a wistful look at the cookie plate. "Well, don't say I didn't warn you," he replied. "When's Bob due in port?"

Mrs. Dinsmore's face relaxed. "Around the twenty-fifth," she said, "he sent me a 'gram. Here, have another cookie. I must think up some little thing to cook for him as a surprise."

The captain snaffled a handful of cookies from the plate and stood up to go. "Your ordinary cooking's good enough for me," he declared, "but, if you mean something like those little shrimps fried in batter you had the last time he was here, go ahead. And watch for that plant." He stalked off across the lawn.

He's getting old, thought Amy Dinsmore, watching the gruff old codger limp around a flower bed (Bjornson had had prosthetic surgery after he lost his foot and, though it had been successful, grafts were never as flexible as natural members), positively old. He ought to see a geriatrician right away. She'd tell him so the next time he came to see her. Talking about Robert that way!

She set the dial on the robot gardener on the front lawn to "Weeding: dandelions" and started along the path that led to the little hothouse where most of the plants Robert had sent her were growing; even in the deep tropics Terra was, with few exceptions, too cold and dry for them. The Martian subjects, on the other hand, were in a psychroplex lean-to, with hygro-scopes and a battery of infra-red lamps to keep the temperature up during the day.

The heavy moist air of the hothouse made Amy Dinsmore pant a little as she entered it—but how *interesting* it was! Even the leaves of her Venusian plants were fascinating, thick and leatherlike, thin and dry and hard like parchment, hanging in heavy serpentine coils or bristling pointed and sharp as so many spears. And their coloring ranged from cerise through a silky taupe and indigo around to an angry bright metallic blue. As for their flowers—oh, my. Amy Dinsmore had never seen anything like them. All you could do was stand in front of them with your mouth open and stare. When she wasn't looking at her Martian succulents, they were her favorites of anything she grew.

She halted in front of the plant Robert had sent her last. Yes, Hjalmar Bjornson was getting definitely senile. How could anybody think that this poor little dried-up thing could be harmful? It was a mere bundle of desiccated stems, with only a tiny new leaf or two to indicate that it was alive. It looked a little better than it had yesterday, though; the colchine solution must have been good for it. Amy brushed a few dead flies from the ledge behind it into her hand and threw them into the composter. She liked to have things neat.

Now, what should she cook as a surprise for Robert? He was fond of sweet things, of course, but it always seemed to her that he praised her meat dishes and entrees most. He liked her cooking so much because her roast turkeys and grilled steaks had a crust on them; electronically cooked food was quick to prepare and it might be as good for you as they said it was, but the outside looked like the inside, and it all tasted flavorless and grey. What was the use of saving time in cooking if you ended up with food that wasn't any fun to eat?

* * * *

"You aren't looking well, Amy," Captain Bjornson said three or four weeks later. He looked at her with the critical attention of an old friend. "You've got on a lot of cosmi-lac, but you still look peaked. What's the matter, worried about Bob? Ships don't get hurt in meteor swarms any more." He looked down at his grafted foot reminiscently. "Not like it was when *I* was a third mate."

Amy Dinsmore shook her head. She picked up one of the brightly-colored hexagons—they had been playing a desultory game of Maroola in the airy coolness of the side stoa—and fiddled with it.

"I haven't been sleeping well," she confessed at last. "I've had such unpleasant dreams. Horrid things."

"What about?" Bjornson asked. "That blasted plant? Honestly, Amy, it looks like some kind of spider to me."

"No! I don't know why you can't leave my Venusian Rambler alone! Robert told me it was a very valuable plant, rare even in its own habitat. It's doing so nicely, too. A spider! I wish you'd stop trying to spoil it for me."

"I'm sorry," Bjornson apologized. "Forget it. Go on, tell me about your dreams."

"Well, on Tuesday—or was it Wednesday?—no, it must have been Tuesday because that was the day after I flew over to Hartford—I was down by the hothouse and I found the most unpleasant thing beside the path." She shuddered. "I've been dreaming about it ever since."

"What was it?" Bjornson urged.

"Oh, a—I guess it must have been a rabbit once. One of the wild ones. Only it was nothing except some fur and some bones. Not decayed, Hjalmar, you understand, just gone. I can't imagine what had happened to it."

"Better see a mental hygienist," the Captain advised after a pause. "Nightmares can be very serious."

"I suppose so. I really dread going to sleep."

* * * *

The next morning, very early, Amy turned on the fluor with unsteady fingers. What a horrid dream it had been! She could hardly believe that it hadn't been real and that she was safe and sound in her own bedroom after all.

Outside, the noise that had wakened her—the jagged, unearthly caterwauling of a couple of tomcats promenading in the moonlight—came again. Ordinarily it was a noise Amy disliked very much—the poor things always sounded as if they were in deadly agony—but now she was glad to hear it. Heavens, if it hadn't been for those cats crying and waking her up, she might still be asleep and dreaming. Dreaming about—about—*blood*....

She turned the ceiling selector to "summer sky," lay back on her pillow, and tried to relax. It was her favorite of all the ceilings her bedroom had, so lovely and calm and blue, and right now she needed something lovely and calm. One thing was sure, she wasn't going to stand this much longer. She didn't believe in pampering herself, but, if she had that dream once more she was going to take Bjornson's advice and see a mental hygienist.

She'd think about something pleasant. Amy tried to fix her mind on her gardening, on how well her plants were doing, but it wasn't a success. When she tried to keep her thoughts on her Venusian Rambler (why did they call it a Rambler?—it was turning into a large, stocky, compact bush more like an outsized Camellia than anything else Amy Dinsmore could think of), they kept veering back to her dream and all that—all that—

Well, then she'd think about Robert. She was a lucky woman to have a nephew like him. She'd worked out several menus, all the things he liked best, but she wished she could think of something a little different. There were so few kinds of meat, when everything was said and done. Lamb and beef and musk ox and bollo and pork. And she always thought bollo was stringy and tough.

Gradually Amy's nerves began to quiet. The cats had grown quiet too, except for an occasional outburst that sounded like lightning made audible. Her thoughts drifted lazily from Robert to her soap carving. After a while she went to sleep....

The morning was sunny and bright, and she felt almost ashamed of herself for having let a dream affect her so seriously. She had finished her matutinal inspection of the hothouse and the succulent growing-shed and had started back to the house when she came on a bundle lying by the hothouse wall. At first she didn't recognize it for what it was, and stooped over it, poking at it with a stick.

After an instant she straightened, nauseated, remembering where she had last seen that ginger-colored fur. The bundle was the not very bulky remains—bones, and some patches of hide—of a cat. Hadn't there been some pieces of white fur too?—of two cats.

She'd better call Hjalmar. It might be dangerous. There must be some wild animal living near her hothouse, a lynx or ferret or wildcat or stoat. Mrs. Dinsmore wasn't strong on zoology, but she knew exactly what sort of an animal she had in mind—something lithe and dark and blood-thirsty. Goodness. It was quite frightening.

On the other hand, Robert would be in port in a couple of days. If she asked Hjalmar to help her, he'd either make an enormous masculine fuss over it (she still remembered the time she'd asked him to put up a towel rack for her and he'd arrived with a set of socket wrenches, a hand electric drill, four pairs of pliers, and a portable arc welding outfit) or he'd pooh-pooh and pish-tush her into silence. Either way, it wouldn't be satisfactory. She'd wait for Robert; Robert was so comforting. If only she didn't have more of those dreams!

* * * *

Despite her apprehensions, her next night's slumber was profound and sweet. She hadn't felt so rested and refreshed in weeks. She put the somni-spray (maybe if she'd thought to use it before she wouldn't have had those horrid night-mares) back in the closet and decided that she'd do some soap carving after breakfast. She felt in the mood for it, and Robert would be disappointed if she didn't have something new to show him that she'd carved since he had last been in port. Besides, she might be able to think of the special dish she wanted to make for him while she was working: she'd found from experience that some of her best culinary ideas came to her while she was making a statuette or plaque out of soap.

The meal concluded, she got out her set of modeling knives and a couple of cakes of soap. Soap was rather hard to get, since most people used synthetic detergents nowadays, but she knew a little store in Perth Amboy that carried it. This last batch had a lovely texture.

Amy rotated the living room on its axis until the light was exactly right, and then sat down in front of her carving desk. What should she make? A statuette? A plaque? A plaque in low relief, a plaque of a flower. Somehow, she didn't want to think about animals right now.

She had sketched in the conventionalized Hermodactylus and was beginning to pick it out carefully from the background when it occurred to her that she hadn't been down to the hothouse this morning to see her plants.

Why, that would never do, she mustn't neglect them, it was terribly important. Important. (Her head hurt; how dizzy she felt!) She'd better go at once, she'd better ... go.... Cake of soap in one hand, knife in the other, panting a little, Amy set out toward her plants in a stumbling run.

She was half-way to the hothouse before it occurred to her to question the impulse which had taken her incontinently from her carving and set her in blind motion toward the hothouse, and by then it was too late. She was no longer a free agent in any sense of the term. The mental grip which had taken the rabbit and the cats to their death had tightened on her inescapably. Remote from her body, in a glassy paralysis of fear and impotence, Amy watched her feet moving briskly down the path.

Oh, if she could only cry out, call Hjalmar! She felt the muscles of her throat straining, but no sound came. And now she was standing before the hothouse, and her hand had opened the door.

The Rambler was waiting for her. Very slowly, like a man flexing his arm, it reached out one of the stocky branches toward her. Amy saw that at the end of the branch, well hidden under the dark green, glossy leaves, was a slender, translucent, hollow thorn. It was about the size of the hypodermic needle the doctor had used when, in her last year's physical examination, he'd taken a sample of blood.

Amy knew exactly what was going to happen. First the hollow thorn, until her veins were dry, and then the slowly opening maw, gaping above the big, swollen, meter-wide base the thick leaves of the Rambler had served to conceal. It would take a long time, but Hjalmar would never miss her before it was too late.

The Rambler's branch moved delicately over the surface of Amy's right wrist, the one with the modeling knife. The other branches were drooping limply away from the purple-pink of its swollen base, waiting, while it hunted the exact spot. It hesitated for an instant and then—Amy's mouth drew into a soundless Oh of pain—struck home.

A dark fluid began to stain the hollow thorn. For just a fraction of a second the Rambler's mental grip on Amy Dinsmore relaxed; she could feel its blind concentration on its own black enjoyment. And in that fraction of a second Amy threw the cake of soap in her left hand straight into the Rambler's fleshy maw.

The Rambler gripped at her mind again, but it was a disturbed and feeble grip. Its branches began to move around the fleshy bole they had shielded, slowly, and then in a furious heaving. The thorn which had entered her wrist was jaggedly withdrawn. Amy, her wrist streaming blood, stared at the Rambler for a moment and then lunged at it with the menacing knife.

* * * *

Sitting outside on the ground beside the hothouse afterward, her forehead on her hands, feeling sick and faint, Amy had an idea. At first she pushed it from her; it was far-fetched, silly, even a little repulsive.

But was it so silly after all? And as to being unpleasant, well, bollo meat commanded enormous prices in the market and, from everything she'd ever heard, the bollo was the very reverse of a fastidious feeder. Even pigs certainly weren't dainty in their eating habits. If she parboiled it in several waters and then braised it slowly, with a hint of ginger in the sauce.... Well, after all, why not?

Amy, the modeling knife in her hand, went into the hothouse again....

... "Gee, Aunt Amy, this meat's good," Robert said. He was talking with his mouth full. "I've eaten indigenous chow on three planets—four, if you call the stuff they serve you on Uranus food—and it's my opinion that there isn't a better cook anywhere in the system than you. Fact. How do you do it, anyhow?"

Amy Dinsmore lowered her eyes. She could feel herself blushing through her cosmi-lac. "Oh ... thank you, Robert."

"She sure is, Bob," Hjalmar Bjornson said expansively. "That gravy! She's the best cook on Terra all the time, but when you're in port she gets sort of inspired."

"What kind of meat is this, though, Amy? And could I have some more?"

"Of course," Amy said. She refilled Hjamar's plate. "It's something new I found in the big auto-market in the city," she said vaguely.

"By the way, Aunt Amy," Bob said, laying down his fork, "after I sent you that plant I heard it was supposed to be carnivorous. I forgot to mention it in my last 'gram. You didn't get into any trouble with it, did you?"

"No, it died," Amy said smoothly. "I had to throw it out. Too bad." She brightened. "Pass your plate, Robert dear," she said.

GARDEN OF EVIL

Originally published in *Planet Stories*, Summer 1949.

Ericson returned to an awareness of his personal identity quite suddenly. He had an impression that it was a long time, months at least, since he had been in a state of normal consciousness. At the back of his mind a memory of pain had imprinted itself as a signet makes an impression in hot wax; he shied away from it. "Where am I?" he asked.

The green-skinned girl squatting beside him in the coppice looked at him sideways out of her dark jade eyes. "Hungry?" she asked.

"But where am—yes, I am hungry. Yes."

Mnathl—he knew, somehow, that that was her name. Didn't he remember her from the other side of the gulf in his memory, from the days when he had begged food in the streets of Penhairn? Mnathl handed him a nicely-roasted *bosula* rib. He ate it avidly. He had always thought the *bosula* was the best of the food animals of Fyhon.

When the bone was gnawed clean she passed him, in a folded fresh green leaf, a mixed grill consisting of bits of *bosula* liver, kidney, tripe, salivary glands, and eyes. He ate that, too. When his stomach was full Ericson lay back with his arms under his head and looked at the big puffy clouds drifting overhead. He had no desire to think about himself or the things that had been happening to him in the last three or four months, but the thoughts came anyhow.

The chief thing was pain—remorseless, long-continued, pain. Mnathl had come to him one day when he was sitting on the dock in Penhairn and told him they were going to Lake Tanais. He had got up and gone with her obediently; a *byhror* addict has little will of his own. The pain had begun after that.

There had been a barren island in the middle of the brackish, poisonous waters of the lake, and most of the time, until just latterly, he had been kept bound for fear he would drown himself in them. Mnathl ... Mnathl had swum over from the mainland to tend him; she had bathed him and kept his body free of sores and vermin, set food before him and tried to coax him to eat. And twice a day she had given him injections of mercapulan with a hypodermic syringe. His arm was pocked with the needle marks. Where had she got the syringe and the drug? She must have stolen them from the big Colony Hospital in Penhairn.

The injections had brought on the pain. Ericson, at the thought, felt sweat break out on his upper lip. What he had endured had been just at the edge of what a man could stand and still live. (His ordeal, had he known it, had been very much less than it would have been had he taken the drug cure in the hospital in Penhairn. Mnathl, though she had not disdained the help of terrestrial science, knew things about the Fyhonese flora and its properties that no terrestrial even suspected. Still, the ordeal had been bad enough.) Ericson shifted his position and sighed.

Mnathl had cured him of *byhror* addiction. In return, he had hated her. There had been weeks, he remembered, when his brain had held nothing but horrible pain and the wish to kill Mnathl. Once, when she had untied him for exercise, he had shammed sleep until she came close to him; then he had caught her by the throat. He had come close to killing her then. And no doubt in those long, maniacal days there had been other times.

Ericson raised himself on one elbow and looked at her. She was pouring water into a clay pot above the small, workman-like fire she had built, and was putting in bits of chopped *bosula* meat. Her greenish skin, the skin of a native of the South Polar continent, glittered slightly as she moved. "Mnathl ..." he said.

She turned toward him quickly, but did not speak. "Mnathl, I'm sorry I tried to ... hurt you on the island. I must have been pretty bad."

Mnathl almost smiled. "No matter," she said. "Pretty soon, soup."

* * * *

The incident seemed to be closed. Ericson lay back in the shade again and watched the movements of the cloud-scape across the deep turquoise of the sky. His eyes felt as fresh as Adam's. The trees were green with the greenness of living emeralds, and the sun had an ardor and a richness like no sun he had ever known before.

Winds blew with caressive, sweet-smelling tendrils over his face, and from the warm soil beneath him he could almost feel strength soaking up again into his body cells. He had visited several planets since he had first left earth; he had loved none of them as he did Fyhon. Fyhon....

Arnaldo, the chunky little head of the paleo-biology department of Penhairn University, had told him once that terrestrials loved Fyhon so because conditions on that planet were like those on Terra during the part of the Cenozoic when man was beginning to become man. Fyhon, he said, appealed to some deep-seated memory in humanity of what a planet ought to be.

Ericson had laughed at him. He was new to Fyhon then, with a temporary appointment as ethnographer to the South Polar Ethnographic Commission. Racial memory had seemed to him as out-moded a concept as spontaneous generation. But his temporary appointment had been extended once, and then once again, and by the end of the second period he had been wildly, hopelessly in love with Fyhon. He had hoped to get a permanent appointment, had hoped to stay on Fyhon for the rest of his life.

Ericson sighed again. After a while he raised one hand above his head and looked at it. He could see the bones and the joints of the bones and the movements of the sinews under the pale gold skin. The marks of Mnathl's hypodermic needle were faintly red. He ran his fingers down his body, surprised at the largeness and hardness of the rib cage, and the prominence of the sockets of his hips. His body felt attenuated and worn. But it was his body, no longer the property of *byhror* and the *byhror* emptiness. He held up his hand once more and looked at it against the light. He was beginning to realize that he was alive.

He drifted off into sleep. When he woke, Mnathl was holding out a steaming bowl to him. "Soup?" she said.

* * * *

They stayed for some eight days in the coppice, while Ericson knotted his memories together. *Byhror* and the need for it were sinking back with the passage of each successive day into the status of things unalterably in the past. Mnathl set snares and hunted—she would not allow him to move a hand—and Ericson watched her almost incuriously. He felt a little more conscious every hour how good it was to be alive.

On the ninth day Mnathl poured water on the cooking fire. She nested the cooking pots together, slung them deftly over her shoulder, and contrived a belt of twisted vines for her hunting knife. "Go now," she announced.

Ericson got up obediently. "Are we going back to Penhairn?" he asked.

The corners of Mnathl's mouth twitched. "No," she said. "Way on up. On in. In Dridihad." She pointed with her thumb.

Ericson stared at her. "Dridihad?" he said. He'd heard the name before. It was ... now wait ... yes, it was the name the natives applied to the heart of the almost unknown South Polar Minor continent. "I can't go there. I've got to go back to Penhairn, now that I'm well. I've three years of *byhror* addiction to make up."

Mnathl's eyes narrowed. "Dridihad," she repeated stubbornly.

"But.... Listen, Mnathl, I'm terribly grateful to you for what you've done for me. I never can thank you enough. But I couldn't go to Dridihad now, wherever it is. I'd need equipment—cameras, notebooks, guns, a tent. Right now I've got to go back to Penhairn, see about getting a job."

"All sorts of things to see," Mnathl said. She edged up to him. "You like. You like good." There was a prick in his arm. Mnathl had made other things in her cooking pots the last few days beside soup.

Ericson felt a peculiar glassy lethargy creeping over him. The sensation was not entirely unpleasant. It was as if he looked at his limbs and his body through a sheet of perfectly transparent crystal. He could see his actions and his movements with absolute clarity, but he had nothing to do with them.

"You like see Dridihad," Mnathl said. "All sorts of things for eth—ethnog—for man like you to look at. Come on. You like good." She started along a shadowy, green-roofed trail.

While Ericson watched with resentful detachment, his body began obediently to follow her. Speech as well as volition had deserted him, and all he could do was to move silently in her steps.

As mile succeeded silent mile, memory and common sense came to his aid. There had been a time, nearly three years ago, when he had set out to explore the periphery of the minor polar continent by himself. His temporary appointment had expired, and he had been moving heaven and earth to get it made permanent. The one-man expedition had been a part of the general heaven-and-earth moving process; it had occurred to him that the Ethnographic Commission might be inclined to view his application more favorably if he could offer the Commission a piece of original ethnographic research, such as a report on the natives in the periphery would be.

His attempt had been a miserable failure; indeed, he owed his former *byhror* addiction to it. His supplies had been eaten by animals, he had poisoned himself with tainted *chornis* liver, fever had attacked him. In his fits of feverish delirium he had thrown away nearly everything, even his hunting knife. In order to get back to Penhairn at all he had had to resort to chewing the leaves of the *byhror* plant. The leaves contain a remarkable stimulant; Ericson had been able to get his fever-racked body back to civilization alive. But it had been at the cost of slavish addiction to the drug.

And now Mnathl—bless her greenish skin and queer flat eyes—was offering him a journey to the mysterious heart of the minor polar continent. Offering it to him on a silver platter. A piece of original ethnographic research. He had been ungrateful and a fool. "You like good," she had said. Well, she ought to know.

The effects of the drug she had pricked his arm with must be wearing off. Ericson found he could smile. "Why are we going to Dridihad, Mnathl?" he asked a little later.

Mnathl shook her sleek green head without even turning around to him. "No," she said.

* * * *

The trip in to Dridihad was a seduction, an enchantment, a bliss. Ericson's strength came flooding back to him. His sick pallor was turning to rich gold. On the second day he whittled, under Mnathl's guidance, a spear and a throwing-stick for it, and on the third and fourth she taught him to set snares and kindle fires with a sliver of *onchian*. The country grew wilder and more beautiful, the trees taller, the sky a deeper blue, the waterfalls more loud. He tried to question the girl, but she never answered anything except "No", and after a little, in his happiness, he gave up asking questions.

What did it matter, after all? He was learning from day to day secrets that any geographer or ethnographer would have given the best years of his life to learn; the piece of original ethnographic research was becoming a reality; and who, except a fool, questions someone who has not only restored him to life but is giving him his heart's desire?

On the eighteenth day, when Ericson's body had filled out and been turned to a living gold by the sun, they came across the pyramid. It stood in a swale with purple flowers growing around it and a small river flowing around one side, and it was so tall that Ericson, looking dizzily up, swore he saw clouds floating around its top. He wanted to stay and look at it, to record it in his mind, but Mnathl was not impressed. She let him have two hours, and then she urged him on.

"But who built it, Mnathl?" he demanded when he had been pulled reluctantly away. "How did it get here?"

Mnathl seemed to be debating whether to answer him. He could never decide whether she was naturally taciturn, or whether she really grudged telling him things. "My people built it," she said at last. "Deidrithes. Long time ago. *Long* time ago." She motioned vaguely with her hand.

Something in the gesture made Ericson see with sudden clarity how deep the abysm of the past, even on this young world with the ardent sun, really was. Fyhon was young; but the Deidrithes had been living on Fyhon a long time.

Two days later Ericson, contrary to their usual custom, was in the lead, breaking trail. Mnathl caught him suddenly around the waist and pulled him back, but she was not quick enough. The huge, thick-bodied snake with the red bandings lashed out at him and just fell short. But one glistening fang grazed his foot.

Mnathl, bleached by fear to the color of an inferior grade of jade, killed the snake with a stone. Then she made Ericson sit down on the grass, and slashed at his foot with her hunting knife.

"What is it, Mnathl?" Ericson asked. The wound was not especially painful, but his heart had already begun to beat slowly and wearily, as if beating were a burden almost beyond its strength, and at the same time it seemed to have grown until it threatened to burst his chest.

"*Outis*," Mnathl answered briefly. She hesitated for a moment. "Bad," she said, as if to herself. "Very bad. Could kill me too." Then she leaned over and set her lips to the bleeding gash her knife had made.

Ericson tried to draw away from her. He was so dizzy that he could hardly see. "No," he croaked, "don't. You mustn't suck it, Mnathl. I don't want you to risk your life."

The green-skinned girl shrugged. "No matter," she answered. "Will do. O.K."

Ericson tried to push her from him, but he was too weak. The world was receding from him in black waves. She sucked blood and poison from the wound, spat, sucked, spat, and sucked again.

He would have liked to protest, to thank her for her sacrifice, but he had no time. His pulse had begun to flutter feebly, and he fainted.

* * * *

For the next several days he was in a stupor most of the time. Whenever he came back to consciousness, he saw Mnathl lying exhausted in the grass near him, and he knew without being told that the poison she had sucked from his wound was moving sluggishly and with slow malignity through her veins. Nevertheless, the wound on his foot was always cleanly dressed and plastered with fresh herbs, and from time to time she opened it with her knife and let the pus escape.

When they were finally on the road to Dridihad again, he tried to thank her for what she had done.

"Anything I can do for you, Mnathl," he wound up with some embarrassment (it is difficult to thank someone who refuses to look at you), "anything I can do for you, why, you let me know. I could have died there, without ever getting my permanent appointment or seeing Dridihad. We're friends, aren't we, Mnathl? Friends." He took her hand.

Mnathl nodded curtly. "O.K.," she said. She pulled her fingers from his. The Deidrithes, Ericson thought not for the first time, were an impassive, unemotional folk.

It took them nearly a month more to get to Dridihad. On the way they had to ford two swollen rivers and beat off the attack of a must-maddened bull *rhodops*. Neither of these incidents had any consequences. On the sixty-sixth day after their departure from Lake Tanais, they came to the foot of Dridihad.

For a week or so the ground had been rising steadily and the air growing crisp and thin. They had labored uphill, uphill. Dridihad itself, built on a high plateau, had been visible for three days before they reached it, a silhouette, faintly pinkish, against the clouds. When they had first caught sight of it, Ericson had felt an almost painful anticipation seize him, and even Mnathl, usually so impassive, had shown, in her glowing face and quickened breathing, how excited she was.

The ascent to the plateau itself, along a path so precipitous that Ericson was always having to clutch it with hands as well as feet, was so toilsome that fatigue had dimmed his curiosity a little when they arrived at the top. Earlier that day Mnathl had thrown the cooking pots and the knife contemptuously over the side of the cliff, and now, cupping her hands around her lips and standing almost arrogantly erect, she strode up to the rosy-red, eroded battlements.

"Klarete laoi!" she called. "Laoi, klarete!" So far as Ericson could see, no one at all was listening. But after a moment the massy doors of the gate began to open outward, ponderously, in the twilight. They went in.

Dridihad, Ericson saw at first glance, was much larger and more populous than he had supposed from below. The low, stepped buildings, all made of the rose-pink stone, seemed to stretch out for mile upon mile, as far as he could see. They made upon him an impression of antiquity so strong that it was almost disturbing. The small greenish people like Mnathl were everywhere. In dots, trickles and rivulets they were pouring out into the streets.

Mnathl's eyes fell on a man near her. She spoke to him. Instantly he bowed profoundly before her, and made a second, shallower obeisance to Ericson.

"Go with him," Mnathl said, turning to the ethnographer. "Sleep in his house." Obediently, Ericson followed his guide. When he looked around toward Mnathl, she had already disappeared.

The man (his name seemed to be Boator) took Ericson to an airy suite of rooms on the top floor of one of the biggest of the houses of red stone. Attendants waited on him with food and drink and water for bathing. They took away his dirt-encrusted, ragged clothing and brought him a heavy greenish robe. After Ericson had bathed and put it on, he inspected himself in the sheet of polished metal that served for a looking glass and decided that the color of the fabric made his curling beard and fair skin look as if they had been cast from yellow gold.

He was tired, but far too excited to rest.

The chief thing, the indubitable, the incredible thing, was that there was a very old, a very populous city, a city whose existence no one had even suspected, in the heart of the South Polar Minor continent. It was news to inflame an ethnographer to the point of hysteria. When Ericson got back to Penhairn with his report, it was going to revolutionize their whole concept of Fyhonese history; one would hardly exaggerate to say that it would be epoch-making news. No doubt there would be a period when they'd consider him the biggest liar since Marco Polo. But after the first skepticism wore off he'd have a permanent ethno-graphic appointment almost forced upon him. His report would shake established reputations, found new schools, would—oh, if he only had something to write on!

When the attendant came in again, Ericson made mo-tions of writing in the palm of his hand, but the man's face remained blank. And when he asked for Mnathl the atten-dant merely shook his head and went out.

For want of anything better the young man hung out of the window watching the smoky flicker of lights in the city around him. It was not until the last one had gone out that he went, reluctantly, to bed.

* * * *

Next morning, immediately after breakfast, Mnathl came to visit him. He hardly knew her at first. The scanty garments she had worn unconcernedly on their journey to Dridihad had been replaced by the stiff, hieratic folds of a dull purple robe embroidered in blue. On her head there was a silvery crown of antique workmanship, set with lu-minous purple stones, and she moved with the conscious dignity of a princess or a priest.

Her manner toward him, too, had changed. She smiled faintly when she first saw him, and everything about her seemed freer than Ericson had seen it before. She was ani-mated, almost vivacious.

He asked her for something to write with. "No," she answered, still with that faint smile, "no use. Hunt now."

They left Boator's house by a side door (to avoid the crowd that would appear at once if they were glimpsed in the streets, Ericson surmised) and entered a small, walled court. There four improbably striped animals, about the size of small ponies, were waiting for them. Ericson mounted one of them, and Mnathl, tucking up her skirts, bestrode another. With two attendants they rode circuitously through Dridihad and out into the high plain.

The variety and abundance of game were amazing. There seemed to be more animals than there were trees, and they came in all sizes, shapes, colors, and coats. There was even a big blue-hued thing that reminded the young man a little of a kangaroo. He enjoyed himself, but he could not help wishing that he knew more about Fyhonese zoology than he did—to appreciate all those properly.

They got back to the city just before dark. Ericson ate, and then Mnathl took him to the temple. It was the tallest building in Dridihad, a stepped pyramid of unusually reddish stone, and Ericson was to grow fond, later, of the view from its flat top. The naos itself, however, was a small room skimpily scooped out of one side of the pyramid, and it was very badly lighted. Ericson, who had resolved, in default of paper to write on, to impress all he saw and heard irremovably upon his mind, had to strain his eyes to see anything.

Mnathl officiated. His first feeling that she was a priestess seemed to be correct. As to the ritual itself, it was highly impressive, especially when one considered that he did not know the language in which it was going on. It ended with the sacrifice of an animal like a *bosula*; while two attendants held it, Mnathl cut its throat, caught the blood in a cup, and poured it on the altar fire. Then she roasted pieces of the meat over the coals and dealt them out among the celebrants of the ceremony, partaking first herself. None of the collops was offered to Ericson; but, then, he could hardly be considered a communicant of the religion of the Deidrithes, whatever it was.

As the days passed, a possible explanation of Mnathl's treatment of him began to come to Ericson. He was not a conceited man, or it might have occurred to him earlier. And it bothered him to think that she was attracted to him, whereas he had never found her attractive in any way. Still, what other hypothesis would account for the facts?

They were together almost constantly and, except for the attendants who were always armed with heavy axes, always alone. She hunted with him, showed him the city, rode with him; she even taught him to play a rather childish game, something like the Sicilian Mora, which she always beat him at. Day after day she took him with her to witness religious rites which were obviously of the most hallowed character. Ericson had the impression that the rites were leading, in a series of slight graduations, up to some supreme event! and he tried to note and remember everything.

* * * *

The climax came suddenly. One lovely evening, just as the full moon was rising, Mnathl took him with her up the steep sides to the top of the pyramid. The two attendants hovered discreetly in the background. For all practical purposes, he and the girl were alone.

Mnathl looked at him. There was a glint, warm, glowing, and facile, in her eyes that he had never seen there before. There was a short but rather embarrassing silence. At last Ericson, feeling like a boor and a churl, took her hand.

"Mnathl," he said, "I'm so grateful to you. You've done so much for me, helped me so much. You ... mean a lot to me, Mnathl." That, at least, was true.

Mnathl pulled her fingers away and regarded him. "What you mean?" she asked blankly. "What you mean?"

"That you ... that I ..." he stopped, too embarrassed to go on.

Mnathl threw back her head and laughed. It was the first time he had ever heard the sound from her, and there was something strange in it. She motioned to the axmen with her hand.

"Not like, not hate," she said blandly. "Let you see, let you hear, so you tell Them all that Deidrithes do. You our messenger. Then we eat."

Then we eat.... For a moment the words echoed meaninglessly in Ericson's mind. The axmen were forcing him to his knees near a depression in the center of the pyramid. "But why ..." he said.

"We hear about you the first time you try trip," Mnathl said. "Everybody know. No other men your color in Fyhon."

His color. Ericson began to understand. Mnathl's devotion, her self-sacrificing tenacity, her long kindness to him, everything—had all been nothing but the prelude to a ritual meal in which his rare blonde body was to be the chief support. No doubt a man of his color would be an especially choice offering to the gods. The gleam he had seen in Mnathl's eyes had been not love, but a kind of religious gluttony.

He began to laugh. Irony had always appealed to him; and besides he was remembering a sentence in the Ethnographic Commission's preliminary survey: "There is no doubt that ritual cannibalism is unknown among the natives of Fyhon."

"O.K., Mnathl," he said, recalling what he had been saved from, what he had seen and learned. "I'm ahead, no matter how you look at it. It's O.K."

He was still smiling when the axman on the right struck and Ericson's severed head went rolling along the surface of the pyramid.

RETURN ENGAGEMENT

Originally published in *Imagination Stories of Science and Fantasy*, January 1952.

"The ingratitude of humans," McBream said broodingly, "is amazing. Loan a Martian a couple of I.U.'s when he's in a spot, and he'll send you greeting cards on the anniversary for the rest of his life. Fish a terrestrial out of the water when he's drowning, and he sends you a bill from the tailor for resurfacin' his suit. Passengers!" McBream spat in the direction of the lucite cuspidor.

I picked up the book from McBream's desk and examined it. It was beautifully printed on outsize sheets of silky preemitex, and bound in smooth, deep-garnet Vellumium. On the spine of the book, in shining miraloy, ran the words, FARQUARSON'S ENCHIRIDION OF EXTRA-TERRESTRIAL COOKERY.

"This what you're so sore about?" I asked.

"Sore?" McBream snorted. "Who's sore? Only petty, small-souled individuals get sore at things. Me, I'm suffering from an attack of righteous wrath. I'm not vindictive, but I hope Farquarson chokes over one of his own recipes."

"The name sounds familiar," I ventured.

"It should be. Farquarson is culinary editor of *Pro Homine*, the super-sharp magazine for men. You must have heard of him. That book in your hand is supposed to be his masterpiece. Masterpiece!" McBream snorted again.

"It isn't as though he hadn't plenty of room for it," my friend continued in an aggrieved tone after a silence. "The first ten pages of the book are taken up with acknowledgments and expressions of gratitude—you know, stuff like, 'My deep thanks, too, are due to Logarithmia McCloy for her skillful and patient typing of this book's manuscript.' And it's dedicated to his hexapod, Waldmeister Schnitzel V. Luftraumzug, 'My six-legged friend and constant companion.' But does he mention Joseph McBream, first mate of the *S. S. Tisiphone*, anywhere in it? Just once? Just one single time? He does not. And yet, if it hadn't been for me that book would never have been written."

"Did you help him with the recipes?" I asked.

"I did not," Joseph returned decisively. "I'm no greasy groon-slinger. The recipes in the ENCHIRIDION—agh, what a flossy way to say handbook—came out of Farquarson's own little head. No, I didn't help him with the recipes. I only saved his life."

"Tell me about it," I said.

"He got on the *Tisiphone* at Marsport," Joseph McBream said, "with a sky-blue hexapod, four robot porters to carry his luggage, and a beautiful blonde secretary who couldn't spell even using phonemes. About half his stateroom was taken up with cooking stuff. He had pressure vats and tenderizers and relayed casseroles, more damned junk than you ever saw outside a museum. He probably had a couple of alembics and an athanor. It was all of it breakable, and the Old Man told everyone on board to be careful of it. Farquarson was some dynast's brother-in-law, and he didn't want to go offending him."

"What was he like personally?" I queried.

"Farquarson? Oh, dignified. God-awful dignified in a loose-jointed intellectual sort of way. He always wore sports clothes and talked with a sort of lazy drawl. His manners were beautiful. Everybody on board hated him.

"The first night out he got into a fracas with the cook about the proper way of barbolizing bollo ribs. Marno, being half-Venusian, was a sort of excitable gesell anyhow, and pretty soon we heard noises like everything in the galley had been thrown on the deck and was being jumped up and down upon. It practically was, too, and though of course all that stuff is made of Fraxex, the bollo ribs got badly burned while the discussion was going on. All we had for dinner that night was clear soup, vigreen salad, and a sweet.

"The second night out of Marsport Farquarson came to my cabin—Johnny and I were bunking together then—and said he had a request to make. He'd been told, he said, that 'spacies' (I wish you could have heard him trying to use slang; it made you feel like there was a skin growing over your teeth)—that 'spacies' had a special drink they, ah, manufactured surreptitiously on certain occasions when they were in space. Its name he, ah, believed, was jet juice. Did we know anything about it? Could we furnish any information concerning it to him?"

McBream paused. His lips had drawn down in a sour grimace. It was obvious that he had become absorbed in memories as unpleasant as a dose of picrin would have been.

"And did you?" I prompted.

"To the everlasting discredit of our common sense, we did. Afterward, when Johnny and I talked it over, we couldn't understand what had got into us. It wasn't as though either of us liked him; and we knew perfectly well how the Old Man felt about jet juice on board his precious *Tisiphone*. We acted like a couple of girls from the satellites all overcome by the glamorous lights of the big space port. Farquarson must have hypnotized us with his fine emporium clothes and his lazy drawl. An' the worst of it was, it was a wonderful batch of juice.

"I don't think I ever made a tastier. It had some bilial berries and kono shoots in it I picked up in Aphrodition, and the usual assortment of Martian fungi and grains. Just before we'd left Terra I'd had an inspiration and I'd put in three mangosteens and a big piece of durian. They were to give it body and depth. Then of course we revved the mixture up with a bottle or two of soma and some cocla extract, and put it away to stew in a dark corner of the hold in free flight, away from the artigravs. It came out a kind of cloudy peach green, smooth as satin and warm and deep and rich. It was a wonderful batch.

"Johnny got a bottle from under his bunk, where he kept it inside his depilitating kit, and poured Farquarson a drink. The old yap tasted it and his eyebrows went up. 'Extraordinary!' said he. 'Ah—could I have some more?'

"From first to last he finished two and three-quarter bottles of the drink. When he went to his little bed that night, he was floating up to his ears. He kept talking about the deadly paididion that was following him, and wanting Johnny to let him come to grips with it.

"The next day the Old Man came down on us like a ton of osmium. He called us up to the bridge and said things that—well, I'm not a young man any more, but they made me feel like I was about fifteen, and Johnny had tears in his eyes before he was done. Then he sent a couple of crewmen into the hold and they smashed the carboy and poured out the juice. One of them told me afterward that there were tears in *his* eyes, too.

"It seems that that black-hearted ape, Farquarson, had woke up with the hangover of the eon. Instead of taking his medicine like a little man, he'd gone loping to the captain for 'remedial agents.' And then, of course, the fat was frying merrily.

"To do Denis (that was Farquarson's first name, Denis) justice, I don't think he realized what he was letting us in for. The 'surreptitious' in the speech he'd made us about jet juice hadn't really registered with him. He probably thought the captain took a kind of 'spacies will be spacies' attitude with us.

"But Zinck fined us each two months' pay and ordered us confined to quarters except for necessary duty until we hit the first of the Rafts in the Ring. The confinement to quarters was all right, bein' disciplinary, but the pay docking, being financial, shouldn't have been imposed without a board meeting, an' we took it up with the union. There was months and months of rowing, and at the end the board affirmed Zinck's fine and slapped another month's penalty on us on its own account."

There was a dispirited silence. "About your saving his life...." I murmured.

McBream brightened. Plainly I had touched on a more pleasant segment of his recollections. The corners of his mouth, which had been austerely turned downward, began to right themselves. "Oh, that," he said.

"In order to know what happened, you got to know what the set-up was. Farquarson had already 'coped with' the cookery of the terra-type planets, and done what he could with the farther, bigger ones. It's pretty hard to get chummy with the inhabitants of Jupiter, even if their food was adapted to human digestions, and I notice Farquarson has only three Jovian dishes in his book. But anyhow, he was finishing up with the fringes, the cookery of the satellites, and he'd booked passage on the *Tisiphone* because we touched at so many of them.

"Like I said, he was related to some dynast with a lot of tug, and the Old Man, after checking with an inspector at Marsport, agreed to let him have the use of the yellow life craft when he wanted it. It was sort of against regulations, but not too much.

"The craft's bein' yellow was important. Conformably to regulations, all the *Tisiphone's* life craft were painted in the psychological primary colors, to make assigning personnel to them for evacuation easier, and all of them carried two paint bombs to 'provide adequate means for prompt renewal of said paint, pigment, enameloid, or tint.' You want to keep your eye on those paint bombs, because they come into the picture later on.

"Well, Farquarson got along all right on the first couple or so satellites. He didn't speak anything except terrestrial languages, which was rather a handicap, and there never were any interpreters. He laid the fact that he was sick as a dog three or four times from things the natives gave him to eat, to difficulties of communication. Myself, I thought somebody got annoyed with the trick he had of looking down his nose and bleating 'Oh, rea-l-ly?' every few minutes, and decided to take direct action.

"Anyhow, he was still in pretty good condition when we got to Iapetus. Iapetus is under a universal dome. The first day he spent mooching around the port and buying things in native markets, but the next day he asked for the life craft and started off by himself. We didn't think he'd get into any trouble. He wasn't the soul of tact, of course, but the Talipygians are usually a pretty mild bunch, good-tempered and fond of a joke."

"Talipygians?" I asked.

"The secondary inhabitants of Iapetus. You can't photograph them easily, because they're partly electrical energy, and they're practically impossible to describe. They look like big maroon hedgehogs, as much as anything, with erectile electric crests over their heads, and lots of white sharp teeth.

"We were having supper on board the *Tisiphone* when Sparks came in and spoke to the Old Man. He'd happened to be running over the afternoon wire on the reproducer, and he'd come across Farquarson's call for help. The blasted idiot hadn't sent it in code, which would have automatically set up alarm signals, he'd just yelled 'Help!' into the 'phone a couple of times, and he hadn't even thought to give his position when he did it.

"Well, I got sent. In a way, it was a logical choice, because I knew as much as anybody on board about the Talipygians. Extra-terrestrial anthropology's always been a sort of hobby of mine. The beauteous blonde secretary was having hysterics and the hexapod was howling its head off in sympathy when I left. Just before I zoomed, Zinck said something in a stern voice about expecting me to return with Farquarson alive and in good condition, or he'd consider it a breach of discipline. He knew I didn't like him.

"I had a real devil of a time finding Denis. We get in the habit of talking as if a planet were about the size of California, and a satellite no bigger than an amusement park. Take it from me, that's nothing but pure woola wash. A satellite the size of Iapetus seems as big as Terra itself when you're hunting a small object on it, and that life craft was only about five meters long. Iapetus has mountains and rivers and woods and ravines and all sorts of stuff. I had object detectors, of course, but Iapetus has lots of ore-bearing rocks, and anyhow, detectors are of very little use unless you're near the thing, and I had no idea where it was. I put in nearly fourteen hours hunting before I found the craft, and even then it was just luck that I stumbled on it.

"It was down in a gully on the edge of some woods. Everything looked peaceful and quiet, and Farquarson wasn't anywhere about. I hovered for a while and thought it over, and then decided to land.

"I had side arms, of course, but I wasn't planning on using them. For one thing, Farquarson might just have turned his ankle and considered it a catastrophe which warranted sending a call for help, and for another, the Talipygians are protected by interplanetary law. They've been classified as a 'non-humanoid species of limited intelligence,' and that means that if you bother one of them all hell pops loose. Quite right, too." Joseph's manner was solemn. "The non-human species of the system are one of our greatest natural resources.

"But as I was saying, I decided to land. I came down easy on quarter-jet, got out, and started toward the yellow life craft. I heard a noise in the brush and turned to look. And the next thing I knew, there I was inside the life craft with my head aching like I'd been drinking eagle spit.

"I figured out later that one of the Talipygians had knocked me out with a discharge from his erectile electric crest. They hardly ever do it, because it's a psychic drain on them, and I'd overlooked the possibility of it.

"Farquarson was inside the craft, looking dignified and distressed. His hair was rumpled up and his nethers had completely lost their press. 'I'm glad you've come, Mc-Bream,' he said as soon as my eyelids began flutterin'. 'Perhaps the two of us can contrive some way out of this predicament.'

"I sat up moaning and holding on to my head. It hurt so much my eyes felt crossed. I could just make out, on the port side of the life craft, a cooking pot with a mess of some reddish stuff in it. My side arms, by the way, were gone. That's one of the things that makes me wonder if that phrase 'limited intelligence' in the description of the Talipygians is entirely justified.

"Anyhow, I helped myself up by pulling on the back of the pilot's seat. Farquarson watched me, his expression intellectual and lugubrious. 'What's been happening?' I asked.

"He shook his head. 'I don't quite know,' he answered. 'I landed the life craft in this spot, picked a quantity of an unknown deep red fruit, and was just trying it out in a dish to which I thought it would be suitable, when I discovered that I was surrounded by a number of large purple animals. They looked threatening. I managed to call 'Help!' into the receiver, and then I was knocked unconscious. Stunned.

"'When I recovered consciousness, I found that the craft had been disabled and the means of communication were gone. The animals, McBream, are still surrounding us.'

"I tottered over to a viewing port and looked out. What I saw made my blood run cold. The Talipygians were bumping around the life craft in a circle, sliding on their behinds the way they always do, and from time to time one of them would rear up and sort of shake his crest. It didn't look so alarming in itself, but as I said, I know a few things about the Talipygians, and that dance or whatever you'd call it is the thing a poetically minded anthropologist christened 'The Prelude to the Sacrifice.' I told you the Talipygians had lots of teeth.

"'I can't imagine why they attacked me,' Farquarson said in a querulous voice. 'I was only engaging in cookery.'

"I couldn't imagine, either. Usually all the Talipygians want is to be left alone. Then I had a sudden wild idea. I stumbled over to the cooking pot and looked in it. Heaven help us! Do you know what that double-barreled fool of a Farquarson had selected to cook?"

"No," I replied.

"A bunch of Tomato Babies."

McBream obviously expected me to be impressed with this piece of information. I struggled with it for a time and then gave up. "I never heard of them," I said.

"Never *heard* of them? What do they teach you kids on Terra nowadays? Why, when I was going to school we had course after course in extra-terrestrial subjects, and you couldn't graduate unless you got at least a passing grade in Solar History. No wonder people are only half-educated these days!" McBream sounded outraged.

I had been thinking. "Wait, now," I said, "it seems to me I read a piece in a digest about the Tomato Babies a couple of years ago. Yes, I do remember. It was by a professor of Folklore in Ares City College, and he said that the myth of the Tomato Baby proved that the folklore theme of the external soul—you know, like the stories in Grimm about the giants who can't be killed because their souls are in magical eggs or crystals—that that theme was system-wide."

McBream looked at me. "It isn't a myth," he said with a hint of indignation, "it's perfectly true. The Folklorist who wrote that article didn't know what he was talking about. The Tomato Babies are a big red ovoid fruit that grows on floppy vines in a few odd places on Iapetus. They're hollow inside, and the Talipygians put their souls in them."

"*Hunh?*"

"Well, more or less their souls. You remember I told you the Talipygians were hard to photograph because they were partly electrical energy. When one of them is sick or wounded, the others take his soul out—the electrical part of him—and put it inside one of these fruits. The Tomato Babies, as far as we can find out, are a sort of natural Leyden jar. Or maybe more like a storage battery. Anyhow, the point is that a sick Talipygian doesn't have to suffer for months and months while he's getting well. His electrical component is popped into one of these containers, and his body can devote itself quietly and painlessly to the business of recovering."

"And you mean Farquarson cooked—?" I asked, boggling.

"Yes. Of course after the containers had been destroyed, the electrical charge was lost. It wasn't quite as bad as murder, because the Talipygians say that when their personal electrical charge is released, it reshapes itself into a higher form; all the same, Farquarson had wiped out twenty or thirty relatives and friends of the beings who were bumping around outside the life craft in their sacrificial dance. When the electrical charge is dissipated, the bodies wither away. No wonder the Talipygians were sore.

"I wobbled back to the viewing port and looked at them. I'd always thought they were quiet, harmless creatures, for all their nearly human size; now they seemed to be all teeth. I'd never realized before what particularly vicious lower jaws they had.

"The thing to do was to try to get into communications with them. Now, I don't speak Talipygian. In my opinion, nobody does, though you'll meet a few space rats who'll tell you they could write a grammar of it. But the traders on Iapetus have worked out a system of conventionalized signs, noises, and so on, for talking to the Talipygians, and it works well enough most of the time.

"I began trying to attract their attention, making burp noises and wriggling my hands. For a long time they went on just as if they didn't notice me. Then one of them, a faint shade bigger than the rest, left the circle of bumpers and came and stood in front of me. His teeth were bigger, too. (I say 'his' but it might have been 'her' or 'its'—all I could really be sure of were the teeth.)

"At first I tried to apologize and explain. The Talipygian listened for a while and then made the noise that means 'No.' He wasn't interested. Then I tried threatening. I told him there'd be space cruisers hunting us, punitive expeditions, all that sort of thing. He didn't say anything at all this time, but I had the impression he was bubbling over with laughter inside.

"He was perfectly right, of course. Humanoid citizens of the system are supposed to know their rights and liabilities in dealing with non-humanoid species. If Farquarson had got into trouble with the Talipygians, it was strictly his own lookout. Under the circumstances, if they carved us up, all the government would do would be to send regretful letters to the names in the 'whom to notify' spaces in Farquarson's and my dossiers.

"Bribery was the idea I got next. I turned my pockets out for trinkets and attractive junk. I waved a hunk of fossilized edelweiss and one of those 'Halmjin' crystal games that were so popular last year in his face. No soap.

"The Talipygian flapped his flippers, erected his crest, and said 'gunk' a couple of times. That meant, why bother? He'd get all of our belongings anyhow after we were dead.

"Finally I asked him what they were planning to do with us. Eat us, the answer came back like a flash. Of course I'd known it before, but it still was a little disconcertin'. I'm not quite sure, but I think he said he was sorry I'd get eaten along with Farquarson. He couldn't help it, though.

"I went back inside the life craft and sat down to think. I was dead tired from all the work I'd put in hunting for Farquarson earlier, and my head still ached. And Farquarson kept dancing around me asking idiotic questions and wringing his hands.

"I pulled out of my mind all I'd ever heard about the Talipygian character, and went over it. It wasn't much. They were said to have mild, peaceable natures, lay eggs, engage in ritual dances now an' then as a prelude to slaughtering the local animals, and be fond of a good laugh. The mild and peaceful nature wasn't much in evidence just at present; the eggs weren't relevant; *we* were going to take the place of the local animals in the sacrifice, and how did the sense of humor help? I couldn't tell them funny stories in sign language, could I?

"As far as that went, I'd only seen a Talipygian amused once. That was when we were in port on Iapetus on the trip before. A fat Venusian had been comin' down the steps of the Tashkent Import and Export Exchange. He'd slipped on the top step and gone all the way down to the bottom, touching only the third and eighteenth steps on the way. It had been quite spectacular. Of course he'd had to go to the hospital afterward and have five stitches taken, but the Talipygian couldn't have known that at the time. Maybe it wouldn't have made any difference if he *had* known—I had a feeling that his people liked their humor practical and rough.

"Farquarson came up to where I was sitting with my head in my hands, and nudged me. 'They're moving faster,' he said in a nervous tone. 'Those things on the tops of their heads are flashing more and more frequently. Do you suppose it means anything?'

"I went over to the port fast, and looked. Just as I'd feared, it meant all too much. Judging from the sign, the Talipygians were getting ready to make ritual hash of us.

"I tell you, I was desperate. Of course we could, and would, make a rush for it, but there were forty or fifty of them to two of us; we were unarmed, and each and every Talipygian could deliver a stunning electric shock. I could feel my mind giving off loud clicks like a Geiger counter near a rich source. What to do, what to do? Then my eyes lit on the rack holding the bomb with the yellow paint.

"Inside two minutes I had all the clothes off Farquarson except his sliskin shorts. At first he was too surprised to complain, even though he turned out to have a considerable paunch. But when I took the paint bomb and began paintin' big bright daisies on his shoulders, back, and tummy-tum, he started to heat up; and when he found out what my idea was, he really did get talky and obstreperous. 'I won't do it,' he said vigorously, 'I absolutely refuse. Not before these animals. Have you no conception, McBream, of dignity? I'd rather—' he glanced out of the port toward the toothy Talipygians and winced a little—'I'd rather be dead.'

"I tried to be reasonable with him. 'Listen, Denis,' I told him, 'it's absolutely immaterial to me whether they eat you or not. In fact, I'm all in favor of their cutting you up in little pieces for a mess of shis-kebab. It would be the finest thing to happen to the System since the discovery of Alpha-Omega power. Yet juicer!' (My feelin's overcame me a little when I thought of all the trouble Farquarson had got me in.) 'But if they eat you, they eat me too, for a side dish, and we can't have that. On your way! Get!' I had to give him a push or two, but he got."

"A push?" I queried. Joseph's narrative was becoming interesting.

"With my foot. It was all to the good, I think—it limbered him up. Well, we went outside the life craft, hesitated a second or so, and went into our dance.

"I was prepared to do my part. I'd painted big yellow flowers all over myself too, and I didn't mind how big a fool I looked, provided it saved my life. But it was plain right from the start that Farquarson, reluctant as he was, was the star of the show. The Talipygians hardly noticed me. They stopped bumping almost immediately and clustered around Denis with their crests popping off and on like space port signal lights.

"That guy really had talent. The idea of him writing a cook book with a fancy title when he could perform like that! After he got started he jumped up and down like one inspired, and once when he fell down, probably accidentally, you could have heard the noise the Talipygians made applaudin' with their flippers on the other side of Iapetus. Funny! Why, he'd have made a fortune on the stereo. All he needed was a little well-timed encouragement."

"Encouragement?" I questioned.

Joseph cast down his eyes. "Well, you know," he said vaguely, "things.... After a while the Talipygians themselves got the idea, an' whenever Farquarson showed signs of slowin' down they shot long, slow, low-voltage sparks out of their electric crests at him. One missed him once and hit me instead; it was just like being stuck with a long, sharp pin.

"Pretty soon Farquarson got so warm the daisies on his tummy began runnin'. The Talipygian chief gooped and guggled and geeked at me until I got the idea and fetched the bomb and painted them on real bright again. I had to renew his daisies three times before we got out of there."

McBream's expression was smug and self-satisfied. He looked like a weetareete which, having finished a jug of bovula cream on one side of a theo table, knows that there is another jug, equally full and equally accessible, on the other side.

"But what finally happened?" I asked.

"Well, the blue and green life craft from the *Tisiphone* came after us. Zinck was on the blue one himself—he thought it was that important. Farquarson was doin' splits and then jumpin' high up in the air, almost to the dome, when they got there. The daisies on his tummy were good and bright.

"Zinck got out of the blue craft, trying hard to keep from smiling, and presented his compliments to the head Talipygian. They glooped and gunked for a minute or two, an' then any remainin' signs of a smile disappeared from Zinck's face. For the trouble was this. The Talipygians didn't want to let Farquarson go.

"The conversation went something like this: Zinck: 'Gloop. Wheepie. Geet.' Intricate wiggle of hands.

"Talipygian: 'Nee. Neeeeee.'

"Farquarson: 'What is happening, McBream?'

"Me: 'Be quiet.'

"Zinck: 'Gleeed! Damn it, Gleeed!' (turning to us) 'They say they're going to hold him as recompense for all their relatives he murdered.'

"Farquarson: 'It was purely an accident!'

"Zinck: (sourly) 'You should have been more careful, Mr. Farquarson, really you should—'Gleep. Wheepies. Blee.'

"The upshot of the matter was that Zinck negotiated a contract with the Talipygians. They agreed to release Denis on condition—" here McBream seemed to be smacking his lips—"on condition that he return on the same date each year and perform for them. His costume, it was expressly stipulated, was to be the same, includin' the daisies.

"Farquarson didn't cut up as rough about the terms of the contract as I'd expected him to. I think he had the idea that a contract between a human an' a non-humanoid species wouldn't be legally binding. But when we got back on the *Tisiphone*, Zinck explained to him that such contracts are always made between the human on the one hand and the Interplanetary Government, acting for the non-humanoid species, on the other. Bindin'! It was more bindin' than a barrel full of nuclear-bond glue."

"And does he—?" I murmured after a silence.

"Yes, every year. He'll be leaving for Iapetus day after tomorrow for his annual pilgrimage. He always gets a lot of bon voyage gifts. Funny, isn't it? He begged Zinck and me—especially me—to keep the terms of the contract quiet, and Zinck said he would. But like I said Farquarson always gets a lot of bon voyage gifts and—isn't it odd?— they're always flowers. Baskets and baskets and baskets of daisy flowers."

The corners of McBream's mouth, which had been somewhat elevated, began to turn down again. "But isn't it ungrateful?" he said indignantly. "After I saved his life and all that! Wouldn't you think mere elementary decency would have made him mention me in his book?"

"H'um," I said.

THE AUTUMN AFTER NEXT

Originally published in *Worlds of If Science Fiction*, January 1960.

The spell the Free'l were casting ought to have drawn the moon down from the heavens, made water run uphill, and inverted the order of the seasons. But, since they had got broor's blood instead of newt's, were using alganon instead of vervet juice, and were three days later than the solstice anyhow, nothing happened.

Neeshan watched their antics with a bitter smile.

He'd tried hard with them. The Free'l were really a challenge to evangelical wizardry. They had some natural talent for magic, as was evinced by the frequent attempts they made to perform it, and they were interested in what he told them about its capacities. But they simply wouldn't take the trouble to do it right.

How long had they been stamping around in their circle, anyhow? Since early moonset, and it was now almost dawn. No doubt they would go on stamping all next day, if not interrupted. It was time to call a halt.

Neeshan strode into the middle of the circle. Rhn, the village chief, looked up from his drumming.

"Go away," he said. "You'll spoil the charm."

"What charm? Can't you see by now, Rhn, that it isn't going to work?"

"Of course it will. It just takes time."

"Hell it will. Hell it does. Watch."

Neeshan pushed Rhn to one side and squatted down in the center of the circle. From the pockets of his black robe he produced stylus, dragon's blood, oil of anointing, and salt.

He drew a design on the ground with the stylus, dropped dragon's blood at the corners of the parallelogram, and touched the inner cusps with the oil. Then, sighting carefully at the double red and white sun, which was just coming up, he touched the *outer* cusps with salt. An intense smoke sprang up.

When the smoke died away, a small lizardlike creature was visible in the parallelogram.

"Tell the demon what you want," Neeshan ordered the Free'l.

The Free'l hesitated. They had few wants, after all, which was one of the things that made teaching them magic difficult.

"Two big dyla melons," one of the younger ones said at last.

"A new andana necklace," said another.

"A tooter like the one you have," said Rhn, who was ambitious.

"Straw for a new roof on my hut," said one of the older females.

"That's enough for now," Neeshan interrupted. "The demon can't bring you a tooter, Rhn—you have to ask another sort of demon for that. The other things he can get. Sammel, to work!"

The lizard in the parallelogram twitched its tail. It disappeared, and returned almost immediately with melons, a handsome necklace, and an enormous heap of straw.

"Can I go now?" it asked.

"Yes." Neeshan turned to the Free'l, who were sharing the dyla melons out around their circle. "You see? *That's* how it ought to be. You cast a spell. You're careful with it. And it works. Right away."

"When you do it, it works," Rhn answered.

"Magic works when *anybody* does it. But you have to do it right."

Rhn raised his mud-plastered shoulders in a shrug. "It's such a lot of dreeze, doing it that way. Magic ought to be fun." He walked away, munching on a slice of the melon the demon had brought.

Neeshan stared after him, his eyes hot. "Dreeze" was a Free'l word that referred originally to the nasal drip that accompanied that race's virulent head colds. It had been extended to mean almost anything annoying. The Free'l, who spent much of their time sitting in the rain, had a lot of colds in the head.

Wasn't there anything to be done with these people? Even the simplest spell was too dreezish for them to bother with.

He was getting a headache. He'd better perform a head-ache-removing spell.

He retired to the hut the Free'l had assigned to him. The spell worked, of course, but it left him feeling soggy and dispirited. He was still standing in the hut, wondering what he should do next, when his big black-and-gold tooter in the corner gave a faint "woof." That meant headquarters wanted to communicate with him.

Neeshan carefully aligned the tooter, which is basically a sort of lens for focusing neural force, with the rising double suns. He moved his couch out into a parallel position and lay down on it. In a minute or two he was deep in a cataleptic trance.

The message from headquarters was long, circuitous, and couched in the elaborate, ego-caressing ceremonial of high magic, but its gist was clear enough.

"Your report received," it boiled down to. "We are glad to hear that you are keeping on with the Free'l. We do not expect you to succeed with them—none of the other magical missionaries we have sent out ever has. But if you *should* succeed, by any chance, you would get your senior warlock's rating immediately. It would be no exaggeration, in fact, to say that the highest offices in the Brotherhood would be open to you."

Neeshan came out of his trance. His eyes were round with wonder and cupidity. His senior warlock's rating— why, he wasn't due to get that for nearly four more six hundred-and-five-day years. And the highest offices in the Brotherhood—that could mean anything. Anything! He hadn't realized the Brotherhood set such store on converting the Free'l. Well, now, a reward like that was worth going to some trouble for.

Neeshan sat down on his couch, his elbows on his knees, his fists pressed against his forehead, and tried to think.

The Free'l liked magic, but they were lazy. Anything that involved accuracy impressed them as dreezish. And they didn't want anything. That was the biggest difficulty. Magic had nothing to offer them. He had never, Neeshan thought, heard one of the Free'l express a want.

Wait, though. There was Rhn.

He had shown a definite interest in Neeshan's tooter. Something in its intricate, florid black-and-gold curves seemed to fascinate him. True, he hadn't been interested in it for its legitimate uses, which were to extend and develop a magician's spiritual power. He probably thought that having it would give him more prestige and influence among his people. But for one of the Free'l to say "I wish I had that" about anything whatever meant that he could be worked on. Could the tooter be used as a bribe?

Neeshan sighed heavily. Getting a tooter was painful and laborious. A tooter was carefully fitted to an individual magician's personality; in a sense, it was a part of his personality, and if Neeshan let Rhn have his tooter, he would be letting him have a part of himself. But the stakes were enormous.

Neeshan got up from his couch. It had begun to rain, but he didn't want to spend time performing a rain-repelling spell. He wanted to find Rhn.

Rhn was standing at the edge of the swamp, luxuriating in the downpour. The mud had washed from his shoulders, and he was already sniffling. Neeshan came to the point directly.

"I'll give you my tooter," he said, almost choking over the words, "if you'll do a spell—a simple spell, mind you—exactly right."

Rhn hesitated. Neeshan felt an impulse to kick him. Then he said, "Well...."

Neeshan began his instructions. It wouldn't do for him to help Rhn too directly, but he was willing to do everything reasonable. Rhn listened, scratching himself in the armpits and sneezing from time to time.

After Neeshan had been through the directions twice, Rhn stopped him. "No, don't bother telling me again—it's just more dreeze. Give me the materials and I'll show you. Don't forget, you're giving me the tooter for this."

* * * *

He started off, Neeshan after him, to the latter's hut. While Neeshan looked on tensely, Rhn began going through the actions Neeshan had told him. Half-way through the first decad, he forgot. He inverted the order of the hand-passes, sprinkled salt on the wrong point, and mispronounced the names in the invocation. When he pulled his hands apart at the end, only a tiny yellow flame sprang up.

Neeshan cursed bitterly. Rhn, however, was delighted. "Look at that, will you!" he exclaimed, clapping his chapped, scabby little hands together. "It worked! I'll take the tooter home with me now."

"The tooter? For *that*? You didn't do the spell right."

Rhn stared at him indignantly. "You mean, you're not going to give me the tooter after all the trouble I went to? I only did it as a favor, really. Neeshan, I think it's very mean of you."

"Try the spell again."

"Oh, dreeze. You're too impatient. You never give anything time to work."

He got up and walked off.

For the next few days, everybody in the village avoided Neeshan. They all felt sorry for Rhn, who'd worked so hard, done everything he was told to, and been cheated out of his tooter by Neeshan. In the end the magician, cursing his own weakness, surrendered the tooter to Rhn. The accusatory atmosphere in the normally indifferent Free'l was intolerable.

But now what was he to do? He'd given up his tooter—he had to ask Rhn to lend it to him when he wanted to contact headquarters—and the senior rating was no nearer than before. His head ached constantly, and all the spells he performed to cure the pain left him feeling wretchedly tired out.

Magic, however, is an art of many resources, not all of them savory. Neeshan, in his desperation, began to invoke demons more disreputable than those he would ordinarily have consulted. In effect, he turned for help to the magical underworld.

His thuggish informants were none too consistent. One demon told him one thing, another something else. The consensus, though, was that while there was nothing the Free'l actually wanted enough to go to any trouble for it (they didn't even want to get rid of their nasal drip, for example—in a perverse way they were proud of it), there *was* one thing they disliked intensely—Neeshan himself.

The Free'l thought, the demons reported, that he was inconsiderate, tactless, officious, and a crashing bore. They regarded him as the psychological equivalent of the worst case of dreeze ever known, carried to the nth power. They wished he'd drop dead or hang himself.

Neeshan dismissed the last of the demons. His eyes had begun to shine. The Free'l thought he was a nuisance, did they? They thought he was the most annoying thing they'd encountered in the course of their racial history? Good. Fine. Splendid. Then he'd *really* annoy them.

He'd have to watch out for poison, of course. But in the end, they'd turn to magic to get rid of him. They'd have to. And then he'd have them. They'd be caught.

One act of communal magic that really worked and they'd be sold on magic. He'd be sure of his senior rating.

* * * *

Neeshan began his campaign immediately. Where the Free'l were, there was he. He was always on hand with unwanted explanations, hypercritical objections, and maddening "wouldn't-it-be-betters."

Whereas earlier in his evangelical mission he had confined himself to pointing out how much easier magic would make life for the Free'l, he now counciled and advised them on every phase of their daily routine, from mud-smearing to rain-sitting, and from the time they got up until they went to bed. He even pursued them with advice *after* they got into bed, and told them how to run their sex lives—advice which the Free'l, who set quite as much store by their sex lives as anybody does, resented passionately.

But most of all he harped on their folly in putting up with nasal drip, and instructed them over and over again in the details of a charm—a quite simple charm—for getting rid of it. The charm would, he informed them, work equally well against anything—*or person*—that they found annoying.

The food the Free'l brought him began to have a highly peculiar taste. Neeshan grinned and hung a theriacal charm, a first-class antidote to poison, around his neck. The Free'l's distaste for him bothered him, naturally, but he could stand it. When he had repeated the anti-annoyance charm to a group of Free'l last night, he had noticed that Rhn was listening eagerly. It wouldn't be much longer now.

On the morning of the day before the equinox, Neeshan was awakened from sleep by an odd prickling sensation in his ears. It was a sensation he'd experienced only once before in his life, during his novitiate, and it took him a moment to identify it. Then he realized what it was. Somebody was casting a spell against him.

At last! At last! It had worked!

Neeshan put on his robe and hurried to the door of the hut. The day seemed remarkably overcast, almost like night, but that was caused by the spell. This one happened to involve the optic nerves.

He began to grope his way cautiously toward the village center. He didn't want the Free'l to see him and get suspicious, but he did want to have the pleasure of seeing them cast their first accurate spell. (He was well protected against wind-damage from it, of course.) When he was almost at the center, he took cover behind a hut. He peered out.

They were doing it *right*. Oh, what a satisfaction! Neeshan felt his chest expand with pride. And when the spell worked, when the big wind swooped down and blew him away, the Free'l would certainly receive a second magical missionary more kindly. Neeshan might even come back, well disguised, himself.

The ritual went on. The dancers made three circles to the left, three circles to the right. Cross over, and all sprinkle salt on the interstices of the star Rhn had traced on the ground with the point of a knife. Back to the circle. One to the left, one to right, while Rhn, in the center of the circle, dusted over the salt with—with *what*?

"Hey!" Neeshan yelled in sudden alarm. "Not brimstone! Watch out! You're not doing it ri—"

His chest contracted suddenly, as if a large, stony hand had seized his thorax above the waist. He couldn't breathe, he couldn't think, he couldn't even say "Ouch!" It felt as if his chest—no, his whole body—was being compressed in on itself and turning into something as hard as stone.

He tried to wave his tiny, heavy arms in a counter-charm; he couldn't even inhale. The last emotion he experienced was one of bitterness. He might have *known* the Free'l couldn't get anything right.

* * * *

The Free'l take a dim view of the small stone image that now stands in the center of their village. It is much too heavy for them to move, and while it is not nearly so much of a nuisance as Neeshan was when he was alive, it inconveniences them. They have to make a detour around it when they do their magic dances.

They still hope, though, that the spells they are casting to get rid of him will work eventually. If he doesn't go away this autumn, he will the autumn after next. They have a good deal of faith in magic, when you come right down to it. And patience is their long suit.

THE DANCERS

Originally published in *Planet Stories*, January 1952,
under the pseudonym "Wilton Hazzard."

It was the hour before dawn. In the middle of the night the big ship had landed on the new planet, the satellite of the sun Proxima. Now they sat in the dark waiting, and they talked.

"I wish we hadn't killed them," Rossiter said softly. His profile was faintly visible against the diffused light of the stars. "It's a bad sign, a bad start for a new life."

"They attacked us," Bernard answered quickly.

"Two spears, against forty blasters and stun guns?" Rossiter laughed. "An attack! We should have met them with stunners at low charge. But McNess ordered us to blast. The woman and the baby stick in my craw."

"All our nerves were on edge," Bernard answered thoughtfully. "I know I was afraid when we first stepped out of the ship. There was something terrifying about air, and space, and the sky. But you're right, of course. We shouldn't have been ordered to blast." The two men were sitting a little apart, but there was a murmur of many low voices around them as the others from the *Elpis* waited and talked.

"I wonder why they attacked us?" Bernard went on. "Primitives usually run. We must have been an unbelievable sight to them, spiraling down out of the sky."

"I don't know," Rossiter replied wearily. "And we can't ask them. They're dead, all five of them. That wind's cold." He was shivering.

"You could go back inside the ship," Bernard said half-humorously.

"I'm sick of the *Elpis*. We all are. Eight years of it—it's too much. We'll get used to the wind, I suppose. There's going to be lots of wind, with so much water and only this one land mass on our new world. It's not like Earth."

Bernard made an involuntary movement. Then he re-laxed. "I suppose the taboo is lifted now that we've land-ed," he said heavily. "We can talk about Earth again, and wonder, and speculate. I wonder what they're doing now on Earth."

"Starving. Freezing. Burrowing into the ground for coal and warmth. They must be living a good many hundred feet down now, those that are left. And the seas are frozen. There's an ice sheet from pole to pole.

"We astronomers paid you back finely, didn't we, Bernard, for all the appropriations you got us in committee meeting. You were always generous with us and the physicists. But when the catastrophe happened, the mystery, the debacle, we couldn't help. We didn't know the answer. We didn't know."

"I remember—" Bernard answered, choking a little, "—I remember the day before it happened. There was a report on my desk about some tribe of Indians high in the Andes. The report said that the parents had been persuaded to send their children to the school in the foothills, that even among the adults illiteracy and ignorance were being eliminated. It was the last of the ignorant tribes.

"I looked up at the sign over my desk and read the mot-to, 'There is nothing unknowable. There are only things not yet known,' and I thought, 'Yes, we're getting near our goal. We've conquered ignorance and superstition and illiteracy. And as time goes on we'll know more and more things. The area of the unknown will constantly diminish. Knowledge is like an expanding circle of light that eats into the darkness.' Then the darkness came. And you didn't know."

"We know what happened well enough," Rossiter corrected. He sounded older than his fifty-two years. "I was at the observatory that night. I remember thinking that it was almost time for me to go to the dormitory to sleep. It was summer; Sirius and the sun would both soon be up. Sirius rose, blazing in the darkness, and after him Leo, in the southeast. It should have been invisible in the sunlight. I couldn't believe what I saw. And still the sun didn't come up.

"We know what happened in a way. We don't know how or why. The sun, our sun, never rose. The sun just disappeared."

"How softly everyone's speaking," Bernard said irrelevantly. "It's the sky and the darkness. I could hardly hear you." He got to his feet.

"Where are you going, Tom?" Rossiter asked.

"I want to look at the bodies. The people we blasted, I mean."

"That's morbid. Don't go, Tom. Stay here."

"But I want to go. I'll be back." He moved away through the dimly visible outlines of men and women seated on the ground.

He came back after a while and sat down by his friend in silence. "I think I know why they attacked us," he said after a pause.

"Why?"

"I think we interrupted some magical or religious rite. They were at a very low level of material culture, of course. The points on the spears were stone, and they were wearing garments of what looked like some sort of tree bark. Not woven cloth. But the young men were wearing rattles of some sort of shell around their ankles, and the old man was holding a little drum in his hands.

"You see, they had a good cranial capacity. As soon as human beings can think at all, they start trying to impose their will on the universe. I think they met here by the shore to perform some sort of magic. The woman and the baby watched, the old man played his drum, the two young men sang and danced. Perhaps this bit of the coast was sacred to them. Perhaps, when we set our ship down here, we profaned a sacred place."

"The woman and the baby bother me," Rossiter said thoughtfully. "It seems a dreadful thing to me to kill a woman. Ever since Kate died...."

Bernard rested his hand for a moment on the older man's shoulder in sympathy. "It was wrong. We shouldn't have done it," he responded. "But we must forget it. Tomorrow, when it's light, we'll bury them."

"I wonder if they were the only humanoid life on the planet," Rossiter said, pursuing his own train of thought "This island was the only land mass we found anywhere. If those five, so few.... When we blasted them, did we wipe out the planet's native humanoid life?"

"Possibly," Bernard admitted uneasily. He cleared his throat. "If they hadn't attacked us we could have helped them. They were primitive, superstitious, blankly ignorant, of course. But they had good skulls. They could have learned. We'd have taught them, as we did the primitives on Earth. We'd have led them gently away from their superstition and ignorance. As we did on Earth. Let's not talk about it any more."

Rossiter made a sort of noise. Bernard leaned forward quickly. "What's the matter, Dick? Are you all right?"

"I—what you said—" Rossiter seemed to grope for words. "Be quiet a minute, Tom. I want to think. What you said then—I—it—" He laid his hands over his eyes.

"I'll get Dr. Ferguson," Bernard offered.

"No, I'm all right." Once more he fumbled for words. "I've suddenly come to understand. You made me understand—*as we did on Earth.*"

"What—"

Rossiter got to his feet. In his normal voice, which sounded very loud in the darkness, he said, "I know what made the sun go out."

The murmur of low talking ceased suddenly. There was a sense of listening, of half-seen bodies leaning forward intently in the starlight. Rossiter said, "On Earth there was always somebody dancing."

"Dancing? I don't see—" Bernard spoke in wonderment, but there was an odd, apprehensive note in his voice.

"There was always somebody dancing," said Rossiter. He halted. Then he continued in a stronger voice, "Always, in the high mountains there was somebody fasting and praying. Always before dawn there was the sound of the rattles and the stamping footsteps.

"In the winter the flame leaped high on the rock through the swirls of snow as they made fire magic. They danced. They prayed. They chanted. And the sun came up."

"What are you trying to say?" Bernard demanded. He had risen and was standing facing the older man.

"That people used to think, before we taught them better, that they had something to do with the sun's rising. They grew too wise to believe it any longer. But who knows? Who knows whether they were not right? Whether the force that impels the stars is not, finally, the human will?"

There was a silence. Somebody laughed nervously.

Dr. Ferguson had already stepped forward and was holding Rossiter by the elbow. Together, he and Bernard urged the older man toward the *Elpis*. They spoke to him gently. They did not argue or disagree with him. They led him inside the ship.

Much later Bernard came out alone. Dr. Ferguson had remained with Rossiter, quieting him with sedatives. It was still quite dark.

Bernard looked up at the sky, sighing. "How long the dawn is in coming," he said, as if to himself.

THE VANDERLARK

Originally published in *Planet Stories*, January 1952.

"Are there any more of them?" Alice asked McFeen when he came back from two hold.

"Yes."

Alice's mouth opened in a soundless O. Her hand went to her breast. After a moment she picked up the comb and began pulling it again through her brittle hair. "How many more?" she asked.

"I didn't count them. Hyra are hard to count. Quite a lot."

The comb caught on a tangle. Alice put it down unsteadily. "I wish we'd never brought them," she said abruptly. "I wish we'd never started on this trip. I hate those things. They're uncanny. They give me the creeps. What do you suppose is making them increase like that?"

"I don't know." McFeen's lean, ill-humored face was more than usually morose. "Listen, Alice...."

"Well?"

"That isn't the worst of it. I found a hole in the mesh of their cage."

"You're trying to frighten me," Alice said pitiably after a second. "There couldn't be a hole in beryllium mesh."

"There was, though. I had to patch it up the best way I could. And ... and ... Alice, there was an eroded spot in the side of the hull."

"You mean there was a spot eaten into on the side of our ship?"

"Yes. I plated it over with the auto-weld. It was near their cage."

The comb snapped in Alice's hand. She stared at McFeen. "I told you!" she said finally. Her voice had risen several notes. "I told you it was dangerous! You wouldn't listen to me. You knew everything.

"When I said maybe there was a reason why the Biologic Survey wouldn't release any Hyra to fight the blight on Varro, you said the Survey was nothing but a bunch of fat-cat office-holders who had to make a lot of fool regulations to look like they were earning their salaries. You talked big about how it was your duty to help the poor bosula ranchers on Varro fight the blight. You tried to pretend money wasn't the reason why you were smuggling the Hyra out to them. You knew all the answers, everything would be all right! Oh, you were Mr. Know-it-all!

"Now we're in deep space with an eroded hull. In deep space! I told you something would happen! I to—"

McFeen slapped her hard across the mouth. "Keep that gabby trap of yours shut," he said threateningly. He hung over her menacingly for a moment. And then, relenting (after all, he and Alice had been through a lot together), "Stow it," he said. "No matter whose fault it is, complaining isn't going to help us now. We've got to figure a way out of this."

Alice put up one hand and fingered her swelling lips. She nodded. "Yes," she whispered, "I guess we have."

McFeen began to walk up and down the little cabin. "The way I figure it," he said, frowning, "is, this is the first time anybody's had any Hyra in deep space. They were all right as long as we were in the system; it wasn't until we hit deep that they began to increase. The deeper in we go, the faster their rate of increase is.

"Hyra come from Pluto, and when the Biologic Survey tried them out on germs of the blight from Varro and found they controlled it, the tests were made on Terra. Still inside the system, I mean. And under system conditions Hyra increase so slowly that for one to bud off was a real rarity.

"The way I figure it, conditions are different out here in deep. Maybe it's because inside the system there's always some gravity. Even off the planets, I mean. We don't notice it, but it stands to reason it must be there. When there's no gravity at all, the Hyra start to breed. And when they breed they give off a ... a kind of gas, or something, that attacks beryllium."

"But we've got gravity on the ship," Alice said through her swollen lips. "We don't go floating around."

"It isn't really gravity, Alice, it's just from the centrifuge."

"Oh. Well, if it isn't, what is real gravity?"

"I don't know exactly," McFeen confessed. "I never was good at theoretical stuff. Some kind of electro-magnetic force, I guess."

Alice nodded uncomprehendingly. "Couldn't we—couldn't we get rid of the Hyra, Mac?" she asked timidly. On impulse she put out her hand and touched his sleeve. "We could think up some way of killing them if we tried, I guess. You're awfully smart. And then we could start back home. I'm so scared, honey. Those Hyra scare me so."

McFeen turned on her fiercely. "You blasted fool," he said, "don't you know how it is with us? Is something the matter with your head? I've been blacklisted. There isn't a place in the system I could get a job. There isn't a man in the system I could borrow money from. If this trip fails I'm sunk, done for, finished. Get rid of the Hyra! You brainless, blathering idiot! Do you want to starve?"

Alice shrank into herself. "But, Mac—"

"If we can get through to Varro with the Hyra we've got, the big bosula groups will make us rich. We can have everything we've ever wanted. Now shut up."

He went to a locker and began getting equipment out of it. Alice watched him, running her tongue over her swollen lips. "What are you going to do, Mac?" she asked at last.

"Rig up an electro-magnet around the Hyra," he said without turning. "It might help. It's got to help."

It didn't work. Whether or not McFeen's theory was at fault, the apparatus he rigged up around the cage of Hyra did no good. He tried chemical solutions, sprays, hard and soft radiations—nothing helped. He took to spending most of his time in two hold, trying desperately, with the help of the auto-weld, to keep the eroded patches on the hull under control. Without telling Alice, he made experiments designed to "get rid" of at least some of the Hyra. These too failed. The silicious, gelatinous bodies of the Hyra were extremely hard to destroy. Short of methods which would have endangered the whole ship, there was nothing he could do.

McFeen's natural moroseness was changing rapidly into an inflammable desperation when, quite abruptly, the increase of the Hyra stopped. At first he was incredulous. He tried over and over to count those in the cage, and gave up in disgust. More convincing was the evidence of the hull; no more eroded patches were appearing. For some twenty-four hours he held on to his incredulity; then he allowed himself to be conquered by relief.

He went to Alice with the news and found her as incredulous as he had been. He had to take her into two hold and show her the hull's gleaming, intact sides piece by piece before she would be convinced. Then she began to giggle in hysterical relief.

"Poor old Hyra," she said, "poor old things. I guess I was pretty mean about them, Mac. I'm sorry. Poor old things!" She looked toward the crowded Hyra cage and then, rather hastily, away again. "But everything's going to be all right now, isn't it, Mac? Now they've stopped increasing, everything's going to be all right."

"You bet it is," McFeen said expansively. "Nothing more to worry about. Say, listen, Alice...."

"Yes?" She was still looking obliquely toward the Hyra cage.

"What do you say we go back to the cabin and have a little drink? To celebrate."

"That's a swell idea," Alice answered warmly. "I always said you were smart, Mac. Let's go celebrate." She glanced once more toward the Hyra and then followed him out of the hold.

* * * *

Back in the cabin, McFeen broke out a bottle of soma concentrate. He and Alice drank it slowly, with much inconclusive speculation as to the reason why the Hyra had ceased to breed. When the soma was gone, McFeen brought out a bottle of phlomis. Usually he and Alice began to quarrel bitterly when they reached the second bottle in their drinking bouts, but this time they were both feeling too good for it to happen. They went on from bottle to bottle, drink after drink, in a thickening haze of moist, maudlin goodfellowship. Finally they both passed out. Meantime the ship slid on and on into the deep.

McFeen awoke some ten hours later with his sinuses thundering. Liquor always did that to him. He had a dim, uncomfortable feeling that at some point in their drinking he had insisted on telling Alice what he had really done with the 1,500 I.U.'s she thought had been stolen. Even more faintly he seemed to remember her responding with a full and equally indiscreet account of how she had spent the three months he had been on Uranus. Oh, well, it didn't really matter. Neither he nor Alice was the kind of drinker who remembers details.

He sat on the edge of his bunk for a moment, gathering strength, and then groped his way over to the aid chest. He got out two sobrior pills and swallowed them. As his head began to clear, he looked around for Alice. She was lying on her back in her bunk, snoring heavily, with a long strand of her bleached blonde hair lying across her face. She'd be out for a while yet, he guessed.

Meanwhile, he'd better go see how the cage of Hyra was. It was always possible that they'd begun to breed again. Or was he feeling too queasy to look at them now? Any tendency to queasiness was bound to be increased by looking at Hyra. No, he'd better not put it off. Still walking rather unsteadily, he left the cabin and went into two hold.

His first impression was that the Hyra cage had grown. Surely it was much larger than it had been. Then he realized that the size of the cage was unchanged; it seemed larger because it was emptier. There were fewer Hyra in it than there had been before.

There were no visible holes in the mesh. It was impossible. McFeen, cold sober now, knelt down beside the cage and inspected the mesh centimeter by centimeter. Everywhere it was whole and unbroken; he didn't think a flea could have got out through it.

He turned on the floodlights and gave the hold an equally thorough scrutiny. No, no Hyra. Not a Hyra anywhere.

Leaving aside the question of how they had got out through the mesh, where had they gone to? Number two hold, like the others, was hermetically sealed. And he knew no Hyra had gone past him when he had broken the seal on entering. The whole thing was impossible. He must be imagining it. After all, he hadn't counted them.

McFeen leaned against a bulkhead and pressed his fingers to his head. The pain in his frontal sinus was jumping again. Maybe he was still a little bit buzzed. He didn't think he was, but it was possible. That would account for a lot.

He looked at the cage once more. Wait, now, he had it. The reason it looked so much emptier was that the Hyra (ugh, how he loathed them—he'd never let Alice see how much) were all jammed together at one end, heaped up on one another, like a pile of oozing, pupilless eyes. Naturally the cage looked bigger when the Hyra were piled up like that. McFeen almost laughed in his relief.

He sealed the hole up carefully and went back to the cabin, his footfalls ringing unevenly. Alice was sitting up in her bunk. She had washed her face and pushed her hair out of her eyes. She nodded shortly at him when he came in. After a while she got up and began opening some soup.

* * * *

They both felt better when they had eaten. Alice revived sufficiently to comb her hair and spray some make-up on. The pain began to die away in McFeen's head. He'd been a fool to get so excited over nothing. All the same, he was going into the hold and have another look at the Hyra. He pushed back his chair.

"Where you going, Mac?" Alice asked. She was gathering up the remains of their meal and putting them in the disposer.

"Two hold."

"They aren't increasing again, are they?" she asked in quick alarm.

"No, nothing like that."

This time there was no possible doubt. The heap of Hyra was less than half the size it had been. In the time since he had left the hold—certainly not more than three-quarters of an hour—it had gone way, way down. He could count the Hyra without any difficulty now. There were either sixteen or seventeen.

McFeen's heart began pounding wildly. His chest felt so constricted he could hardly breathe. For a moment he tried to fight his panic, to reason with himself. Then he turned and ran for Alice.

She came rather unwillingly, understanding from his hoarse incoherence only that the Hyra were not increasing any more. Even when she saw the almost empty cage she was not alarmed. "Why, honey, there must be a hole there you haven't found," she said reasonably. "A hole or some—" she fell silent suddenly.

"Mac," she said in a quite different voice.

"Hunh?" McFeen had been trying to count the Hyra; it seemed to him that there was one less in the cage than there had been when he went to the cabin just now for Alice.

"Mac, where's that shadow coming from?"

The fear in her voice infected McFeen with instant irritability. "What shadow?" he demanded. "What are you talking about? Haven't we got trouble enough? Be quiet! What are you starting in on shadows for?"

"Mac...." Alice had to swallow and lick her lips before she could go on. "Look at it. There. In the corner of the cage." She pointed with one hand.

McFeen's eyes followed the gesture. For an unbeatable moment he looked squarely at the thing in the corner of the cage. His heart gave a horrible lurch, like a horse trying to unseat the rider on its back. "It's nothing," he said desperately. "Nothing, nothing! Just a shadow. The bulkhead's casting it."

"Was the shadow here when you were in the hold before?"

"I don't know. Yes, of course it was. It must have been."

Alice stood quite motionless for an instant. Her elbows were pressed to her sides, her hands against her chest, in the feminine posture of resistance and defense. "Turn the floodlights on, Mac," she said.

The lights snapped on. The hold was illuminated from all sides. It was an illumination as shadowless as that of an operating theater, as bright as the noon of a terrestrial day. The shadow in the corner of the Hyra cage was quite unaffected by it.

* * * *

Alice drew a long, quavering sigh. She put both her hands on McFeen's forearm; he could feel her trembling. "Mac, honey," she said very softly, "you know such a lot, you're so smart. Won't you tell me where the shadow's coming from? Won't you please tell me what's making it?"

McFeen looked at her. His eyes were wild. "I don't know!" he said in a high, breaking voice. "I tell you, I don't know! Stop asking me questions! Stop badgering me! I'm getting out of here!" He pulled against her for a moment. Then he tore loose and ran.

"Mac, honey," Alice said when they were back in the cabin once more with the hold sealed behind them, "I think I know what that thing in the cage is." She spoke with surprising calmness. Though she was trembling a good deal she had, all things considered, come out of the hold in better condition than McFeen had.

"There's nothing in the cage," McFeen answered, shuddering. He uncapped a phlomis bottle and drank from it. Drops of the liquor were running down his chin. "There's nothing in the cage."

"Oh, yes ... Mac, I think it's a Vanderlark."

He put the bottle down. The drink had helped him. "A Vanderlark? What's that supposed to be?"

"I guess there's only one of it," Alice corrected herself. She rubbed her lips for a moment with a handkerchief. "I wish my mouth wouldn't shake," she said petulantly. "It makes it hard to talk.

"The Vanderlark's a—a thing—that lives in deep space. It's made out of black. One of my boy friends who was a pilot in deep told me about it once when he'd been drinking. He was awfully afraid of it.

"I guess it's everywhere, really. Bill said it was everywhere, always, in all spaces and all times. I don't understand that very well, do you, Mac?"

"Go on," McFeen said. He turned the phlomis bottle around, studying it with haggard concentration.

"Anyway, deep is where the Vanderlark is more. Most of the time it doesn't bother anybody. But if you call it—it—it comes."

"Call it? What do you mean? We never called that thing."

"We didn't mean to call it," Alice said, "but maybe.... Or maybe it was the Hyra called it. I mean, when we hit deep space and they began to increase. Maybe when they increased they made a—a quiver in space that attracted it. They're not alive in the way other things are. They're different. Or maybe a part of them has always been where the Vanderlark is."

McFeen rubbed his hands over his face. He got another bottle of phlomis from the locker, uncapped it, and then put it aside without tasting it. "What are we going to do, Alice?" he asked humbly.

Alice stood up, smoothing the folds of her wrinkled dress. In this moment she had an odd dignity. "I'm awfully scared, Mac," she said as if in explanation. "The best thing I can think of is to put the Hyra cage in the life raft. And then jet the raft off away from the ship. Maybe the Vanderlark will follow it. When the Hyra are gone, maybe the shadow will leave us alone."

There were only three Hyra left in the cage. The shadow had filled all except the cage's extreme end. McFeen looked at it and then averted his gaze. His face was so white that the brownness of his skin looked like greasepaint laid on a mask. Alice was standing behind him. He muttered something. He laid hold of the cage and tried to lift it up.

There was an instant's resistance. Then the shadow welled up enormously, in a horrible puffing-out of black. McFeen was left holding the top edge of the cage. All the rest was gone.

He stood looking stupidly at the metal for a moment and then dropped it on the deck. He began to back away. He was screaming on a single high note. He hadn't stopped screaming when, without any perceptible motion, the blackness, the limitless blackness, closed over him.

Alice turned and ran. The life raft was aft of two hold; she couldn't have got through to the raft even if she had thought of it.

She ran from the hold to the cabin, from the cabin into the control room. The Vanderlark found her there, pressed flat against the metal of the prow, mumbling "No no no," over and over and trying to push her way out through the ship with her hands. Quietly and easily it extended itself and made her a part of it.

Then there was silence. After a while the Vanderlark flowed over the whole ship. And then there was nothing there at all but the Vanderlark.